SUBWAY STOPS

For Shanté
From David
Williams

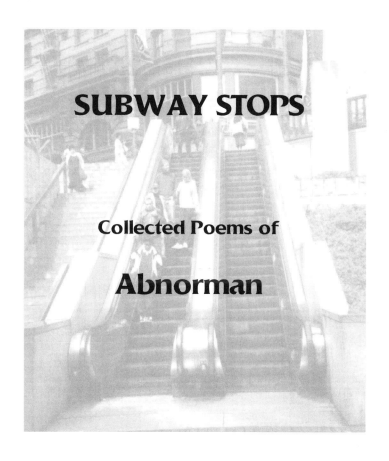

SUBWAY STOPS

Collected Poems of

Abnorman

GLB PUBLISHERS ® San Francisco

FIRST EDITION

Published in the United States by
GLB Publishers
P.O. Box 78212, San Francisco, CA 94107 USA

Cover by W. L. Warner
Cover Photography by Clifford Baker
and W. L. Warner

Publisher's Cataloging-in-Publication

Library of Congress Catalog Card Number: 98-96354

ISBN 1-879194-24-4

First printing October, 1998
10 9 8 7 6 5 4 3 2 1

Many of Abnorman's poems were published first in newspapers in Louisville, Kentucky, and are reprinted here with permission. In *The Lavender Letter*:

"Laughabout" was first published as "If I Had A Wishing Well", Vol. 6, No. 10 (November, 1986).

"The Man That I Am", Vol. 6, No. 5 and No. 6 (May and July, 1986).

"Moonburn", Vol. 7, No. 1 (February, 1987).

"Get Away! Don't Work Me!", Vol. 6, No. 10 (November, 1986).

"A Total Blast", Vol. 6, No. 4 (April, 1986).

In *The Letter*, Louisville, Kentucky:

"De-Mystery (code three)", Vol. 5, No. 9 (October, 1994).

"I'll Take Two of Those and Twelve of Them", Vol. 5, No. 10 (November, 1994).

"Maybe Today", Vol. 6, No. 1 (January, 1995) (in the same month the author died).

"Kentucky Kisses", Vol. 6, No. 3 (March, 1995) (posthumously).

"Haircut", Vol. 5, No. 7 (July, 1994).

"He Shakes Me", Vol. 5, No. 9 (October, 1994).

"River-Minutes", Vol. 5, No. 7 (July, 1994).

"I've Only Got Two More Teeth", Vol. 5, No. 10 (November, 1994).

"Take Off!", Vol. 5, No. 10 (November, 1994).

"May 89", Vol. 5, No. 7 (July, 1994).

"Stud Muscles and Crud", Vol. 6, No. 1 (January, 1995)(in the same month the author died).

"Deadline", Vol. 5, No. 11 (December, 1994).

A POET'S LIFE

by

David Williams

Norman Nichols, who wrote under the pen name Abnorman, was born December 16, 1956 in Louisville, Kentucky and grew up in a working class suburb of that city. Thirty-eight years later and barely ten miles away, he died of AIDS.

Between those brackets, his life was filled with adventure and surprise in places far and near. Perhaps because he had no real plans or goals to speak of, he managed to live a great deal more than most people can ever imagine. He traveled light, leaving little besides his poetry behind.

Norman was a fiercely independent spirit who sought out new experiences often at the expense of caution. In later years, his '72 Nova proudly sported a license plate proclaiming "BURSLF." If any slogan were said to have been his personal motto, it was "Be Yourself." Until late in life he paid little heed to convention.

During most of his adult life he was constantly on the move. After a disastrous stint in the Navy in the mid-1970s, he spent the next fourteen years roaming the country, first to Miami, then Washington State, Los Angeles, San Francisco, Indianapolis, Houston, and finally back to Louisville. If he ever called any place home besides Louisville, it was San Francisco.

At first, life in San Francisco couldn't have been better. When he arrived in 1981, the Castro was at its height. For a good looking man with a tidy income and a curious nature, it was paradise. That the whole scene would come crashing down within three years, no one could have foretold. It was the dawn of AIDS: he didn't have a chance.

Norman's favorite hangouts were in the bar district south of Market, where he wrote some of the poetry in this book. For a while he took to scrawling short verse on bathroom walls, occasionally prompting terse written criticisms from others. Most poems were written in the streets and parks, or at his apartment on the top floor of 471-1/2 Sanchez.

Eventually he drank too deeply of that city's free spirits. By 1985, psychically battered and physically bruised–and perhaps a bit scared by the onslaught of the AIDS epidemic–he concluded reluctantly he'd have to leave if he hoped to survive.

The following five years took him to Louisville, Indianapolis, and Houston, but by 1990 he'd returned to Louisville for good. It was there, in November, he was diagnosed HIV-positive.

Norman took the illness in stride, accepting his fate with a certain wacky gusto. To the astonishment of many, he often proclaimed that AIDS was the best thing that ever happened to him. He meant it had freed him from mundane concerns, allowing him to focus on more important ones, such as the spiritual. His optimism remained boundless. He was even thinking of returning to California for good until we met in the spring of 1991.

Most of the poetry in this book was written during his San Francisco years. Baghdad by the Bay inspired him like no other place. Images from the gay scenes of the day fill nearly every line of his poetry. If his work can be said to belong to one city, it's San Francisco. He loved its sights and sounds, its hyperenergies, and could never get enough.

Norman tended to write in a spontaneous rush, letting the pen race across the page as fast as his thoughts would take it. Not that he wouldn't return to a poem later to change words here and there. He simply didn't care for the conscientious slaving to which most poets find themselves chained. He relished the flash of writing, the *moment juste*. For him, the thrill of writing was more in the creation than in viewing the final product.

His work was little appreciated by most friends and strangers at the time.

Ninety-one poems have survived. This book contains sixty-seven. They are divided into two sections, as Norman envisioned them: *Upper Level*–lighter poems of love, afternoons in the park, and so forth–and *Lower Level*, the dark and sometimes dangerous underculture he dove into in the early 1980s.

His *Upper Level* poems are fun and easy to read, full of air and sunlight. But he poured most of his energies into the *Lower Level*. Those poems are filled with his most startling verbal pyrotechniques. Images of leather sex, heavy drug trips, orgiastic nights, high powered rushes, assorted degradations and tinges of madness tumble across the page.

It was the lower level of life that fascinated Norman the most, even as he understood what a dead end it was. He knew it couldn't last forever; he just wasn't in a hurry to leave it.

Except for the memories his friends and loved ones continue to carry, the best of his life lives on in his poems.

Norman is buried in Louisville's Cave Hill Cemetery at the foot of a black African granite tombstone. A stained-glass flame bursting with all the colors of the rainbow shoots up the center. On the marble pedestal are carved the words by which he lived: "Life is a banquet, and most poor souls are starving to death."

He has also been memorialized by two panels for the NAMES Project, on a plaque of names at Louisville's AIDS Memorial Garden, and in the Circle of Names at the National AIDS Memorial Grove in San Francisco's Golden Gate Park.

The original manuscripts for all his poems are now deposited at the Williams-Nichols Institute, Inc., a gay and lesbian library and archives in Louisville: one of the few gay and lesbian organizations in the world that commemorates the love of two men in its name.

To David Woolums,

First Fan

Table of Contents

Upper Level

Lower Level

UPPER LEVEL

LAUGHABOUT

I wanta do things I can
look back on and laugh about
and still not have a record
and have my peace of mind
and have more laugh-abouts left
than the laughs I've left behind.

DE-MYSTERY (code three)

Anything is possible,
everywhere is hot.
Make-believe is modern
especially when it's not.

At random outlaw images
break through the glass
of dreams.
It just may be
just like it seemed,
except for when it's not.

The wind knows what
and is pickin up,
hey now here it comes.
Get knocked down by the
rush of things and find that

Anything is possible,
everywhere is hot.
Make-believe is modern
especially when it's not.

GRAMMARPHONETICS?

(Parentheses), apostrophes', periods
and colons; I capitălize on mў
complēte parts of thoughts.
Ī fill in my blanks – the write way . . .
. . . AND it's easy → (you don't say!).

THE MAN THAT I AM

Lincoln Logs, Tonka Truck
toys,
Little League and little boys.
And suggestions from
various parts of my Id,
yes, in fact did
make me the man
I am today.

(hey hey)

One bedroom
3 brothers and me.
Hand-me-down clothes,
pass the puberty.
Late at night
we'd cuss and fight,
I was on my way
to the man that I am
right here today.

(hey hey)

I ain't done,
I ain't begun!
I'm changin'
and tomorrow man
is another day.
All right.
Ok.

(hey hey hey)

4

KENTUCKY KISSES

Look somewhere in California
and you'll probably find me there.
Livin' like an earthquake native
shakin' it with savoir faire.

Livin' on the left coast,
way out on the edge
where everything is everywhere
and it's all inside your head.

But sometimes a bluegrass banjo
makes me start to sing.
And I send Kentucky Kisses
back east inside my dreams.

Mom and Dad and all my friends
said they could never leave.
I went and did but Kentucky
went and kept a little bit of me.

Southern accents, you all;
and basketball when winter starts.
That has a special place in that Old Kentucky Home
inside of my heart.

Cause sometimes a bluegrass banjo
makes me wanta sing
and I go home with Kentucky Kisses,
back east inside my dream.

I'LL TAKE TWO OF THOSE
AND TWELVE OF THEM

The drapes are almost closed, but
inside the part that's not I
can see the moon. The master of the
stars who touches the tides
of every sea, whispers down,
"Look at me."

How can I not?
Who could say no to such intrigue?
Just the way I hear it whisper
makes me promise everything.
I bet it gives me what I came for,
desire right on track.
AND, the colors are compatible,
alabaster and black.

I was in the right place
at the right time and
in the right room.
And then the drapes were open
just oh so right
so I could see the moon.

No, I never will be sorry,
I'll never ask for before back.
AND, the colors are two-compatible,
alabaster and black . . .

NO MOW

There's a free-growth area
in my back yard, about 6x7 or
5x6 or something.
When it started it was purple
and now it's all clover
and the dogs walk in it
and the dandelions died.
Sometimes I go there and think.

RIVER-MINUTES

Swimming upstream
(being currently-employed)
two white birdfish
flap their wings
and flip their fins
and a barge goes by,
leaving some-awake.
It disappears.
Birdfish play.

MAYBE TODAY

Perhaps the park,
or maybe the beach.
I can take some
bread for the birds
and a peach for me;
plus one in the bag,
in case I should see
someone with
no one,
at the park
or the beach.

AIN'T IT GRAND?

Went down by City Hall today
and took a nap in
the midst of all that
architecture,
feeling non-political
and nearly at home.

Caught up in the grandeur,
I bet I smiled even
while I
took a nap in
the midst of all that
architecture down by City Hall.
Down by the fountains,
down by the birds,
down by where 32 other
people were taking a nap
in the midst of all that
architecture,
sleeping in the sun
all
alone.

THE BARBER'S CHAIR

Clutching a Reader's Digest, my reflection
danced off 15 mirrors, and each image saw
itself 15 times, and the barber spoke out
from the rear that he'd be only a minute
and to take a chair.

I did sit down, on a halfway comfortable
old swivel seat. The magazine stayed on
my lap and "I AM JOE'S LIVER" stared
at my chin while the barber spoke
out from the rear that he was terribly
sorry and he'd be right in.

He finally arrived, inevitable clippers in
hand, and looking at my nervous hair wanted
to know what kind of cut I'd need.
But as I began he cut me off, talking
like lonely barbers do at a lonely
barber's blurry speed.

His voice rivaled the music of his scissors,
those oral sparks flew from between
his teeth. He began to tell the story
of his many days, as barbers do, and I
was the considerate victim veiled in one
of his blue pin-striped barber's sheets.

He spoke of the navy, sailing away with
his youth, arguing with his uncle on
the destiny of his life. He showed me
photos of his once-burned shop and
informed me that at home was his
surprisingly spirited invalid wife.

11

I just didn't care, I only wanted a
cut, but I smiled and frowned on cue
as he carried on. I thought perhaps
I should let him know I did not wish
to speak, then realized I had said
not even a word. So I slightly sighed
and consoled myself in the fact that from
his barrage I would soon be gone.

He finished around one ear and slowly walked
to the other side; in one of the mirrors I
watched him talk. He suddenly stared at the
side of my head then walked back around
to make another tiny, quick snip. Smiling now,
he spoke of his uncle and his uncle's wife,
how in the 20's they came down the coast,
immigrating from Canada on a Canadian ship.

I wished he would hurry and finish on
up, his story was not interesting to me.
He asked if I were a
merchant marine, as plenty had just
arrived from the cold and stormy
Pacific sea.

I said no.

He trimmed up the back, blocking it
since it had obviously been done like that
before. He looked and cut, stepped back and
cut and looked, then walked to
the front where he talked and cut
some more.

He spoke of the town, Anacortes it was,
and its history, its colorful fishing
and cannery past. The smell of salmon
seeped up through the flooring, or at least
I smelled it while sitting in his chair.
I sat up a little straighter and Joe's liver
flipped over to leak its bile
against the well-worn leather.

Each phrase then flaunted its texture,
no more a meaningless ramble. My
eyes tremored slightly as I felt this
man's life introduce itself through his
barber speech. I began to see
the things of which he spoke, and thought perhaps
I knew his wife at home, in bed. I
wanted to hear it all and I then
grabbed at his words but they
quietly passed just out of my reach.

He stripped off my sheet and spun me
around. My reflection danced off 15
mirrors and each image saw itself 15
times and I paid him $4 plus 1 for
his tip. He smiled and nodded his head.
I sat my hat down upon my hair and
walked back to the dock where just
recently tied up was my
(merchant marine) ship.

He took my money and rang it up,
saying "Thank You" as I walked from
the store. He talks to me still,
long after I've gone,
though he's returned to the rear
in the shadows once more.

HAIRCUT

"I like your head"
she said,
and the subway
began to stop.
I smiled so wide
my ears fell into my mouth
and then
I couldn't hear a thing.

I stayed on
she got off.

I'M PLEADING, INNOCENCE

Come,
let me teach you of innocence.
I have the truth to tell.
Take my hand.
Take my word.
Take a ride. Come on,

Let me teach you of innocence.
I DO have the truth to tell.
Please believe and
come with me.
They won't let me in
if I'm by myself.

HE LOOKS GOOD ALOT

He looks good alot,
He's got face everyplace,
and a smile that swallows the room.
People invite him over
so they can fall in love,
then disappear.

COME LOVE ME

Come love me.
Show to me your deepest dream,
I'll show you mine–look–see.
Love me.

Tired of lies? Sick of deceit?
It's most necessary that you've
tasted these.
If so, I may love you.
But only if you'll also
come love me.

Afraid? good, our fears are
a part of us; deny them not for they'll
be soon subdued and find their place.
Trust that I can love you,
so come to me now.
Come love me.
I love you.
It'll be ok.

I DIDN'T KNOW IT WOULD BE LIKE THIS!!

I wish I could.
I want to.
I CAN.
I am.

OHMIGOD!
OHMIG!
OHM!
O!

HE SHAKES ME

Say, when the very last thing on
my mind is (maybe)
that time at King's Island,
he shakes me.
He comes at me
from behind
and
he shakes me.
Together we relive
those times
and for a bit, I forget
(that I'm alone).

Or, I'll be pouring milk into
a glass
and out of the blue
I start to laugh.
He shakes me.
He comes at me
from all sides and
he shakes me.
And reminds me
that the love we shared
will always be there.

He shakes me,
I laugh.
He shakes me,
I cry.
He'll shake me
until the day I die.

Shake me.

HOW PRESUMPTUOUS

I dance independent, my feet are
free though I'm sure to your
gaze they would seem to be
connected to the rest of me.
As I dance independent my eyes
do too and inbetween kicks
they look and wonder all about you,
there in your chair looking at me
as I dance independent on two
free feet.

So,
I reach out to you and
suggest you be right over here,
dancing, like me.
I spin and leap! You remain in your seat.
Then, inbetween kicks my eyes
watch you smile and
I shamefully see
that you were dancing all along,
independently.

I'VE ONLY GOT TWO MORE TEETH

Slip under my pillow
and slide inside of
my dreams.
Oh, please don't depart,
disappearing by dawn.
Just once, Tooth Fairy,
be a man about it and
wake up with me.

JUST A SCRAPE

I'm stumbling over
my concern for you. But
I really do not care,
I'm not pickin' it up (anymore).

I didn't carelessly
leave it laying around; and you
think it just HAPPENED
to happen the day before your
breakdown?

You think I just HAPPENED
to start walkin'
without falling down?

You is densely populated.
I would NOT recommend a
no-growth period.

TOO TWO

One learns to be, well,
wary,
of speaking too soon
and things,
or sometimes of speaking at all.

I suppose like wine it
comes with age
(I suppose older men do, too).
One just learns to be,
well,
you know,
wary.
One learns not to speak
too soon.
You know what I'm talkin' about.

Yes you do, too.

TENNIS ANYONE?

If only
Could the book be
Changed a little, oh,
Say towards the end?
Just imagine . . .
A totally different
Tuesday the 29th . . .

I can.
Sometimes I do all day.

WHAT'S THE BIGGIE?

Why should anyone worry about the intricacies
of living a life?
So, what's the biggie if I'm older and
single? My poor lonely sperm?
Or if the executive next door
has a blue-collar wife?

Somebody, somewhere once muttered some
pretty odd rules to mandate how
the human life just had to be led.
The majority followed, ridiculing the
spinster back home and the weird boy
with glasses. Ridiculing differences
that "Just won't fit in here,"

they said, "This perfectly round hole
cannot accommodate a square, for the
hole is there and absolutely MUST
be properly sated."
(providing one could see the hole)
Unless you were a round peg
with circular pre-destined
coitus intentions he/she had to wait
and only contemplate it.

My self, I just will NOT censor,
nor fret if I'm an outcast branded.
I live only by ignoring such
meddlesome lives.
And I don't need to comfort my sperm
for lonely it's not
(it has friends over whenever it likes!).

WHERE THE HELL IS VICKIE?

My Dearest Victoria,

I miss you Vicki. Time goes
by so fast and then when I go
to remember sometimes things
seem so long ago.

I can almost hear
your laugh and see that look
in your eye (when ARE you gonna
get another one of those?)

I miss you Vickie.
And that makes me love you
even more.

Where the Hell are you?

OF COURSE I HAVE TIME TO TALK!

Instant coffee, beer in the fridge,
five books from the library.
Sunset out my window, crossword
puzzles in The Times and cigarettes
to smoke. I drink, read, gaze at,
amaze at and put in
ashtrays fat with debris, all by
myself. So, thanks for dialing!

Songs I sing, teeth I brush,
garbage I take out. Clothes I
wash, toilet I flush and
depression I fake out.
I hum and scrub, I discard and
clean, I disinfect and fool
all by myself.
So thanks for dialing!

The beer seems colder, tastes
a little better, while we sit and
speak of things. Your voice
in my ear colors the sundown
and makes it deeper.
A friend in need, I was,
indeed.
So, thanks for dialing!

YES I TOOK MY MEDICINE

I thought about thinking,
but couldn't. Therefore
I thought not, I think.
So I thought about thinking
some more, but
think my thoughts were too
busy thinking about
what I thought of thinking
about thoughts I had not.
(when you think about it,
you're not sure if it was what
you thought. I'm not. And I
thought I knew what I was
thinking about).
I am, therefore I am not.
(I think . . .)

FULL BLOOM

I am awake. Yet I fall
A
  S
    L
      E
        E
          P . . .
And still yet I wake up,
I think.

Though my eyes are
closed (I'm sure they are),
right in front of me
I see
small green trees
growing and growing
and growing, right in
front of my closed (?)
eyes. I see them soar
upward to the sky.
The laughter of the leaves
(so many of them there are)
entices me and it reaches down to carry me away
(temporarily I fear).
The leaves hold me
with their fragility
and they whisper
"Norman – look down."
I do and
see the ground below
as flowers burst forth through
the soil, emerging already in
full bloom.

Never seen such a thing.

They dance in a breeze
that I don't feel.
The leaves whisper
"If you want . . . it's all real."

Guess what?

TAKE OFF!

Fasten your seatbelt,
'cause we're goin' out . . .
oh, say to the
Sea of Tranquillity.

Bet you never thought it'd
be so soon, but
hold on tight
'cause here come the moon!

You know what?
You're a fun date
('course we really do be high).
How 'bout we stay out real late
and see if on the moon
we know how to fly?

I say OK;
You say FINE.

MYSTERY MOVING

I'm a mystery moving,
and I got the plot to where
I'm bulging with clues
and the potential to do
both what a mystery does and
what it does not.

LOWER LEVEL

MOONBURN

I was burned by the moon
– a full moon flame
shot off through the
night
and back again.

Burned by the moon,
a wonderful pain
as it pierced the sky
and changed my name.

Moonburn,
moonburn,
night-time steam
whistle down
on top of me.

Moonburn;
Moonburns and eternity.
Powerful partners,
oh
the moon burned me.

Off in the distance,
deep in the sky,
I (a beast) and shadows thrive.
Fear not the flame
that licks at you,
come love me and
learn of
the burn of the moon.

IN MY ROOM

Boots on the ceiling,
there's someone upstairs.
I know.
I listen from my bed
and
jackoff in the dark
with the shadows there.

Anticipatin, I'm salivatin
over manhood
from an unknown place.
I bet his face is hot
and I bet he's got
promises and everything.

Boots on the ceiling, heart in my hand.
I think I fell
in love last night
while I stretched out in bed
and pressed my lips against
that noise inside of my head.

Someone's there,
I know.
It's what I think,
I hope.

VISION

I had a dream last night and
in it was an orgasm.

Never know what's gonna
happen next, do one?

Shooting stars and reams
of shooting up speed.

I had another dream tonight
and in it was another orgasm . . .
but it wasn't mine.

I DON'T GO TO NO GYM

My idea of lifting weights is
goin' around pickin' up
bad habits.

I'm so pumped up
I'm wanted in
7 states.

STUD MUSCLES AND CRUD

Track marks, tattoos
are a couple of clues,
the crud stud escaped
from Folsom State.
He came to the Haight
in '68
packin crazy wads
with tainted bait.

Got infected points
and stolen joints
he's cocked his trigger
and itchin to fly.
The hurtin he's squirtin
in your arm is no toy,
his eyes roll back
while he shoots you up,
bad drugs and germs
will burn you, boy.

He's runnin loads,
his cylinder holds
a danger dick
screaming for you.
He'll whisper and grunt
and hypnotize you
with track marks and muscles
and scary tattoos.

He made his escape
in late '68
speedin and greasy
and ready for fame.
He found his new point
in yesterday's trash,
now it's up your arm
spittin in pain.

Stud Muscles and Crud,
the ultimate date,
beats off to a beat out back.
You're suckin on track marks,
defective love,
it's ram-jam-jackoff attack.

There is a final burst of heat,
all your mucous membranes swell.
Your biodegradable torso eats
39.2 on the richter scale.

THUNDERFLESH AND SADDLESTUFF

You think nothin's left
but a bunch of crap,
ain't nobody got no guts?
Hey sucker, if you're bored
that bad, it's because you ain't ever had
Thunderflesh and Saddlestuff.

Thunderflesh and Saddlestuff,
can you believe it, man?
Blowin' bad,
heatin' up,
just one look
you'll fall in love
with Thunderflesh and Saddlestuff.

Suck on thunder,
libido fed,
rodeo inside your head.
Like to kiss
when they cuss
duo dick swingin' tough.
Go on down and
get fucked up.
Thunderflesh and Saddlestuff.

GOD DAMN, I'M SAVED!

(Run me)
to church. Get me up a
cruci-fix; make my little
light shine.
Redeem me with a cruci-
fix,
Save Me Jesus, don't got
much time.

Trust me; it's true, I
believe in you. So,
preach to me a cruci-
fix . . .
. . . a quarter-hit will do.

Thank God that I'm a Baptist,
'cause once one does one
always is,
now baptize me, quick, I hold my breath,
cruci-
fix.

(if you don't I think I'll die)

One more time, make me
born again, send me to
the light.
It makes me weep, this need so deep,
but I'm back again, like I was last night.
Got one helluva crucifix.

CRYSTAL MANEUVERS
(divided by 5)

DAMN, DAMN, DAMN IT'S GOOD

Awesome damn steam,
just suck it right in.
Silver bullets and voltage,
incredible wind.

Charge on, Crystal,
your flashtown run
my river's pumpin'
electric blood.
Bolts of lightning
deep in my veins,
push-me-faster –
crystal-waves.

Blood-brother to flames
each time, surprised.
I'm methin' round
I'm crystalized.

Awesome damn steam,
I'm suckin' it in.
Silver bullets and voltage,
incredible wind.

II

NYET, WATERFORD IT AIN'T

I must be steamin'
my vegetables are peelin'.
Speakin' rushin'
but Moscow don't understand
a word I say,
I blow them away.

Got anti-gravity
inside o' my anatomy.
I'm slam-dancin' fast, immigration's flipped.
Hey, no shit,
I'm pistol-whipped.

But the Kremlin says
"Nyet, this man
swears allegiance to quarter-grams."
Fuck you Moscow, you bolshevik rot.
Suck me off,
I'm a cosmonaut!

III

STRANGE EMBRACE

My friend has got
a strange embrace,
mere words
could never name.
It touches me,
deliberately,
it sucked me in effectively.

Please don't stop,
but don't go on,
I'm not some neo-tourist.
I'm not a simple trip

for a complex intense
native
who's bored and laughs out loud
for fun.

It spit directly on my dreams,
labeled them detrimental things
then ridiculed my yesterday.
It chained me down, convincingly,
padlocked it undeniably,
shooting its ego at
point-blank range.

I wonder where I am,
I wonder where I'll be.
What is this strange embrace
exhaling deep inside of me?

I think I love you,
I think I'm scared
of an ingredient
inside my brain somewhere.

IV

BATTEN DOWN THE HALLS OF MONTEZUMA

Thanks to methamphetamine,
some liquid thing that
followed him here from Tennessee,
he is really quite weird
and un-quietly getting weirder.
He shook and insisted
that he really enlisted
but this marine is make-believe.

He took an oath
(he swears he did)
along with a quarter
either tomorrow or today
or august or june
or sometime back when he was 26 . . .

. . . he can't remember
ain't it a bitch
but boy he's proud, cause . . .

. . . he signed up when
times were tough
and shot through boot
in such a rush
he joined espionage
in the tweak brigade.
They train wide eyes to
look for camouflaged
intruders attempting
to impersonate:

the one-armed lady at
the corner store
and every single fuckin
whore, and all the kids
in fifth grade who he
never NEVER saw walkin
this way to school before.

And the coded clicks on the telephone
and the strange people upstairs
with their nervous dog and brand-new
Ford Escort who are
always mysteriously
ALWAYS home
(except for last tuesday or wednesday
when he thinks they were gone).

Since he's the only
one to observe it all, he's
increasingly worried with
what's going on.
But, no one will listen
much less agree, that
whoever they are they went and
infiltrated 1983.
(and if they weren't watching
from right down the hall
he'd take a leak and then
go a.w.o.l.)

Now this marine-gone-wrong,
complete with combat fatigue
suspects his own shadow
got sucked off by an oral

branch of the enemy, in a
battle-of-the-bulge-type-way.

He decides the fate
of all creatures from make-believe
and pulls his gun
and picks at his skin
and tries to swallow
then tries again
and means to try one more time
but forgets and slips into a dream,
spasmedically,
inviting incognito screams to pollinate with
sticky sleep
where they pull the shades, dehydrate
and blame it on reality.

V

I NOW CALL THE SHOTS

I now call the shots,
not some inanimate thing
that laughs at me
while it tap dances and sings and
stomps its feet real hard
in my head wanting me
to run real fast
and keep on running real fast until
I fall down
until I fall down
dead.

There's a con man barkin'
for a motley side-show.
There's a black-out in there
so don't you go
(and pay a quarter to lose yourself
somewhere inside).
You'll bounce around in
neon-darkness,
always alone,
and be another one of those
who keep on bouncing
until they bounce real fast
right out of control.

GOIN' FISHIN'

Around 1:00 every morning
my glands get hot,
then my tongue swells up
and I smell "THE SLOT."
I get it together,
hit up in the kitchen,
grab my boots and
go fuckin' fishin.

I'm committed to my vices
my loins are stuck
on pullin' in the big ones,
I'm fishin to fuck.
Licensed for my nightly
Folsom-Feed,
I'm suckin' on THE SLOT
gettin' ready to eat.

I'm illegal, immoral
and jackoff in my jeans
while I fish and piss
on the pavement and things.

Yeah, my rod is real
and my tacklebox tight.
I'm all grown up
and fuckin' fishin' tonight.

NAKED EYES

Your naked eyes give you away.
So don't you dare make a mistake
and go out with naked eyes.

People lie and change their shape,
a chameleon's trick it's true.
They pretend to sleep when they're really awake,
they say it's gold but it's only fake,
they're looking for a fool.

Silhouettes of shadows are taking aim
for right between your thighs.
You've only got yourself to blame,
guess what Abel got from Cain.
Guess again, go on, fantasize.

Your overt glance sucks on chance,
light the night on fire.
They'll show your dreams a foggy fate
they'll let you go when it much too late.
Dancing fast with their desire.

Your naked eyes give you away.
Don't you dare make a mistake,
don't go out with naked eyes.

FOLS-O-M

Go west, young man,
get down on your knees
out south of market
down on Folsom Street.

Go west young man,
go get high.
One trip will make
you citified.

Be certified citified
get plugged up tight,
just fuck-suck-fuck
all fuckin' night.

No stop signs down here,
just concrete things.
Could be you out here
on Folsom Street.

I'LL TAKE THE BIGGEST ONE YOU GOT

If you gave me a dollar
for every man I've had
I'd go out and buy me
a cadillac.
With am/fm
and a full tank of gas,
if you gave me a dollar
for each piece of ass.

No ifs, no ands, just a lotta
hot butts,
hey, I'm a mechanic man,
fixin up nuts.
And if you gave me a dollar
for each set I've had
I'd give you a ride
in my cadillac.

I've jammed it up the middle,
I've rammed it from the rear,
I've made it fit no matter what.
So just give me those bucks
and climb in back, boy,
I'll drive you home
in my cadillac.

ROLL MODEL

There is just (almost) too
much puberty in that
pair of pants over there.

I'm (almost) havin trouble talkin'.

He is grown up in places
that coming-of-age never went.
So I'll try to button
my jeans and button my lip.

Let me at him, adolescence.
That teenage-boy is mine.

TURN ME LOOSE

Big fat heat in my hands,
you better hold on tight.
Got electric in my pants,
I'm runnin' hot tonight.

If feelin' good is what
you want, I got your
deesires hangin'.
I'll pump 'em up
like really slow,
you'll explode in just a minute.

Turn my eyes boy, you turn
me loose, I'll ravage
you and make you sore.
Set my boot
down on your heart
then stand up (slowly)
and ravage you more.

I'll cram your face so full of heat
your tongue will suck your soul.
I'm packin' heavy sinner-meat
black and blue and full of smoke.

If feelin' good is what
you want, I got
your deesires
hangin'.
I'll pump 'em up,
like really slow,
say "I love you"
and then explode.

BAD HABITS

I got bad habits.
Why, I'm double-daylight savings time
and bankin' on a full moon
that won't be here for 20 years.
I hear 'em bitch,
well that's just too-tough shit,
cause I'm so bad I'm good.

And not just good, but damn good.
I got the best bad habits
around, better than any
most people's only
heard about.
That's me and my bad habits.

Addiction to the rhythm
got a power over me.
It ricocheted then rocked and rolled
and picked up speed –
Why, I'm flyin',
I'm breathless,
hey look at me!
Where'm I at?
Cain't fuckin' see!

I don't mind though,
it's ok;
new bad habits
comin' anyway.
They're here (I smell 'em)
so listen fast
– really, I'm good –
just, my habits are bad.